Dear Parents:

P9-DMI-619

Congratulations! Your child is taking the first steps on an exciting journey. The destination? Independent reading!

STEP INTO READING® will help your child get there. The program offers five steps to reading success. Each step includes fun stories and colorful art or photographs. In addition to original fiction and books with favorite characters, there are Step into Reading Non-Fiction Readers, Phonics Readers and Boxed Sets, Sticker Readers, and Comic Readers—a complete literacy program with something to interest every child.

Learning to Read, Step by Step!

Ready to Read   Preschool–Kindergarten
• big type and easy words • rhyme and rhythm • picture clues
For children who know the alphabet and are eager to begin reading.

Reading with Help   Preschool–Grade 1
• basic vocabulary • short sentences • simple stories
For children who recognize familiar words and sound out new words with help.

Reading on Your Own   Grades 1–3
• engaging characters • easy-to-follow plots • popular topics
For children who are ready to read on their own.

Reading Paragraphs   Grades 2–3
• challenging vocabulary • short paragraphs • exciting stories
For newly independent readers who read simple sentences with confidence.

Ready for Chapters   Grades 2–4
• chapters • longer paragraphs • full-color art
For children who want to take the plunge into chapter books but still like colorful pictures.

STEP INTO READING® is designed to give every child a successful reading experience. The grade levels are only guides; children will progress through the steps at their own speed, developing confidence in their reading.

Remember, a lifetime love of reading starts with a single step!

© 2016 Universal Studios Licensing LLC. "The Secret Life of Pets" is a trademark and copyright of Universal Studios. Licensed by Universal Studios Licensing LLC. All rights reserved.

Published in the United States by Random House Children's Books, a division of Penguin Random House LLC, 1745 Broadway, New York, NY 10019, and in Canada by Penguin Random House Canada Limited, Toronto.

Step into Reading, Random House, and the Random House colophon are registered trademarks of Penguin Random House LLC.

Visit us on the Web!
StepIntoReading.com
randomhousekids.com

Educators and librarians, for a variety of teaching tools, visit us at
RHTeachersLibrarians.com

ISBN 978-0-399-55483-4 (trade) — ISBN 978-0-399-55484-1 (lib. bdg.) —
ISBN 978-0-399-55485-8 (ebook)

Printed in the United States of America

10 9 8 7 6 5 4 3 2 1

Random House Children's Books supports the First Amendment and celebrates the right to read.

THE SECRET LIFE OF **PETS**

MEET the PETS

by Mary Man-Kong

 Random House 🏠 New York

Do you ever wonder
what your pets do
when you're not home?
Meet Max and his friends
to find out.

MAX

Max is one lucky dog.
He lives in New York City
in an apartment building
filled with his pals.

Max loves his owner, Katie,

and waits all day

for her to come home.

DUKE

Duke was adopted
from the pound.
He is Max's new brother.

Duke is excited about his new home,
but Max isn't ready to share.

GIDGET

Gidget loves Max.

She is the sweetest Pomeranian,
but don't let her squeaky voice
and puffy fur fool you.

Gidget would go anywhere
or do anything to save Max.

CHLOE

Chloe is one fussy feline.

Chloe can't be bothered,

unless you have food.

Max is one of her best friends,
even though he's a dog.

MEL

Mel is a friendly pug,
but not when it comes
to squirrels.

He thinks squirrels are
going to take over the world!
Mel chases and barks at them
every chance he gets.

BUDDY

Buddy is short,
long, and awesome.
Mel and Buddy are
best friends.

Buddy and Mel go a long way
to help their pal Max.

NORMAN

Norman is always lost.
This guinea pig travels through
the building's air vents,
looking for his home.

Somehow, he always ends up
at Max's house.

LEONARD

Leonard looks like
a pretty posh poodle.
But Leonard turns up the volume
and becomes a heavy-metal mutt
after his owner leaves.

POPS

Even though Pops needs
a doggie wheelchair,
this old basset hound gets around.
He knows the city like he knows
the back of his paw.

When Max goes missing,
Pops leads his friends
on the search to find him.

SNOWBALL

Snowball is one tough bunny.
Abandoned by his owner,
Snowball vowed revenge
on all humans.

He is the leader
of the Flushed Pets.
These abandoned pets
live in the sewers beneath
New York City.

**LIBERATED FOREVER,
DOMESTICATED NEVER!**

This cat has a bad attitude!
Ozone and his gang rule
the alleys and fight dirty.

They don't like intruders
on their territory.

TATTOO

This tough potbellied pig
got inked by his owners.
They practiced drawing
their tattoos on him.
Now Tattoo works for Snowball
as his faithful second-in-command.

Snowball and his gang rescued
Ripper from Animal Control.
Ripper wears a muzzle because
his bite is worse than his bark.

Derick was flushed
when he got too big.
Now a member of the Flushed Pets,
he is Snowball's backup
on dangerous missions.

BEARDED DRAGON

Bearded Dragon is

a cold-blooded lizard.

He loves to drive cars,

even though he doesn't know how.

He is crazy at the wheel!

Max and his friends
and the Flushed Pets
are all special
and need lots of love.

© 2016 Universal Studios Licensing LLC. "The Secret Life of Pets"
is a trademark and copyright of Universal Studios. Licensed by
Universal Studios Licensing LLC. All rights reserved.

© 2016 Universal Studios Licensing LLC. "The Secret Life of Pets"
is a trademark and copyright of Universal Studios. Licensed by
Universal Studios Licensing LLC. All rights reserved.

© 2016 Universal Studios Licensing LLC. "The Secret Life of Pets"
is a trademark and copyright of Universal Studios. Licensed by
Universal Studios Licensing LLC. All rights reserved.

© 2016 Universal Studios Licensing LLC. "The Secret Life of Pets"
is a trademark and copyright of Universal Studios. Licensed by
Universal Studios Licensing LLC. All rights reserved.

MAX

DUKE

CHLOE

POPS

MEL

GIDGET

BUDDY

NORMAN

© 2016 Universal Studios Licensing LLC. "The Secret Life of Pets" is a trademark and copyright of Universal Studios. Licensed by Universal Studios Licensing LLC. All rights reserved.

© 2016 Universal Studios Licensing LLC. "The Secret Life of Pets" is a trademark and copyright of Universal Studios. Licensed by Universal Studios Licensing LLC. All rights reserved.

© 2016 Universal Studios Licensing LLC. "The Secret Life of Pets" is a trademark and copyright of Universal Studios. Licensed by Universal Studios Licensing LLC. All rights reserved.

© 2016 Universal Studios Licensing LLC. "The Secret Life of Pets" is a trademark and copyright of Universal Studios. Licensed by Universal Studios Licensing LLC. All rights reserved.

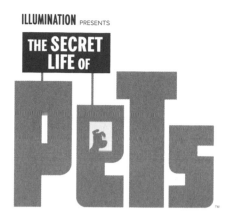

© 2016 Universal Studios Licensing LLC. "The Secret Life of Pets"
is a trademark and copyright of Universal Studios. Licensed by
Universal Studios Licensing LLC. All rights reserved.

© 2016 Universal Studios Licensing LLC. "The Secret Life of Pets"
is a trademark and copyright of Universal Studios. Licensed by
Universal Studios Licensing LLC. All rights reserved.

© 2016 Universal Studios Licensing LLC. "The Secret Life of Pets"
is a trademark and copyright of Universal Studios. Licensed by
Universal Studios Licensing LLC. All rights reserved.

© 2016 Universal Studios Licensing LLC. "The Secret Life of Pets"
is a trademark and copyright of Universal Studios. Licensed by
Universal Studios Licensing LLC. All rights reserved.

SNOWBALL

RIPPER

DERICK

TATTOO

OZONE

BEARDED DRAGON

FLUSHED PETS

METRO PETS

© 2016 Universal Studios Licensing LLC. "The Secret Life of Pets"
is a trademark and copyright of Universal Studios. Licensed by
Universal Studios Licensing LLC. All rights reserved.

© 2016 Universal Studios Licensing LLC. "The Secret Life of Pets"
is a trademark and copyright of Universal Studios. Licensed by
Universal Studios Licensing LLC. All rights reserved.

© 2016 Universal Studios Licensing LLC. "The Secret Life of Pets"
is a trademark and copyright of Universal Studios. Licensed by
Universal Studios Licensing LLC. All rights reserved.

© 2016 Universal Studios Licensing LLC. "The Secret Life of Pets"
is a trademark and copyright of Universal Studios. Licensed by
Universal Studios Licensing LLC. All rights reserved.